Contents

List of characters

Macbeth, *a thane of Scotland*
Lady Macbeth, *his wife*
Banquo, *another thane of Scotland*
Fleance, *Banquo's son*
Duncan, *King of Scotland*
Malcolm and Donalbain, *Duncan's son*s
Lennox, Ross and Macduff, *thanes of Scotland*
Lady Macduff and her son
The Weird Sisters
A gatekeeper
Two murderers
A doctor
Lady Macbeth's maid
Seyton, *Macbeth's servant*

Act One

The Weird Sisters Speak

A Scottish warrior came riding down a rocky track at dusk. He was smiling, and there was blood on his hands from the day's battle. Darkness slowly covered the land behind him, and it seemed he was drawing the night around his shoulders like a great, black cloak. Another man followed, riding hard to keep up, a smile on his face, too.

Macbeth, Thane of Glamis, and his right-hand man, Banquo. Two men who had fought on the same side, and who were friends. For now...

'I've never known a day so foul and fair, Banquo,' Macbeth called out. 'The sun was shining for our victory – but look at those black clouds!'

'You're right, it *is* strange...' Banquo replied.

Suddenly lightning flashed. It revealed three women – the Weird Sisters – waiting at a place where the track crossed the road to Macbeth's castle. They were very old and dressed in rags, and their eyes glowed a fiery red. Thunder rumbled in the distance and echoed off the mountains.

Macbeth and Banquo stopped their horses. Both men were startled and were silent for a while.

'Who... who are you?' Banquo said at last. 'Are you truly human? People that live and breathe and speak?'

'Yes, speak to us, if you can...' Macbeth said quietly, his hand on his sword. He felt that he had fallen under a spell. It was almost as if he had been waiting his whole life to hear what they had to say.

'All hail, Macbeth, Thane of Glamis,' wailed the first Sister.

'All hail, Macbeth, Thane of Cawdor,' wailed the second Sister.

'All hail, Macbeth, who will be king,' wailed the third Sister.

Macbeth caught his breath, and the blood drained from his cheeks.

'What's the matter?' Banquo asked him. 'Surely there's nothing to fear in their words. They're promising you a golden future, a *royal* one...'

Macbeth made no reply. He didn't want to explain his feelings and give himself away.

Banquo turned back to the women. 'Have you no words for me, then?' he said. 'Don't you know what *my* future will be?'

'Hail, lesser than Macbeth, and greater!' wailed the first Sister.

'Hail, not so happy, yet much happier,' wailed the second Sister.

'Hail, you who will not be a king, but whose children will be,' wailed the third Sister.

Lightning flickered once more and their shadows danced.

'Banquo and Macbeth, all hail!' the Weird Sisters wailed.

Macbeth glanced at his friend, but Banquo couldn't take his eyes off them.

'I'm Thane of Glamis right enough,' said

Macbeth after a moment. 'But how can I be Thane of Cawdor too? As far as I know, the man who holds that title still lives. And as for being king – well, that can't happen, either. Who told you to stop us and say such a thing?'

But between two lightning flashes the Weird Sisters vanished.

'Where did they go?' said Banquo. He jumped from his horse and looked around wildly. 'Were they really there – or are we dreaming?'

'Even if we are, I wish they had told us more,' said Macbeth. He turned to stare at his friend. 'Your children will be kings, Banquo.'

'And you will *be* king,' replied Banquo, meeting his gaze.

'Wait, I hear someone coming!' hissed Macbeth.

A pair of riders was racing towards them. They drew their swords ... but Macbeth relaxed. 'It's Lennox and Ross,' he said.

'Greetings, mighty Macbeth!' said Ross.

He and Lennox jumped down from their horses. Both men were thanes themselves and servants of Scotland's King Duncan, like Macbeth. 'The king knows of your great victory in battle, and of all that you did to beat the rebels and save his kingdom.'

'They say you fought like a demon – and that you cut the rebel leader in two!' said Lennox.

'And to show you just how pleased the king is,' said Ross with a grin, 'he told me to call you... Thane of Cawdor. For that title is yours.'

'What? Can this be true?' muttered Banquo, astonished.

'But... the Thane of Cawdor is alive, isn't he?' said Macbeth.

'For the time being,' said Lennox. 'We know now that he supported the rebels all along. The king has sentenced him to death and now wants to see you. We're to take you to him immediately.'

Macbeth and Banquo looked at each other. Then Banquo took the two men aside to find out more. Macbeth was left in the gathering darkness. He slid from his saddle and stood alone, thinking.

The Weird Sisters had promised he would be Thane of Cawdor, and it had happened. So did that mean their other promise would come true? A terrifying idea slipped into his mind, although he hardly dared think about it. There *was* a way of becoming king. He could kill Duncan and seize the throne. Macbeth felt the hairs on his neck stand up.

'My lord, we're waiting,' said Banquo, breaking into his thoughts.

'Er... yes, of course...' stammered Macbeth. 'But I must send a message to my wife with the news...'

Macbeth and Banquo got back on their horses and rode with Ross and Lennox to the king's camp. It was full of battle-stained, tired warriors. But they still cheered their hero

Macbeth as he galloped by.

The king was outside his tent, talking to his eldest son, Malcolm. The rest of his thanes were standing nearby with Donalbain, Duncan's other son.

'Has the former Thane of Cawdor been hanged yet?' asked Duncan.

'Yes, father,' said Malcolm. 'He wanted you to know he was sorry for what he'd done, and begged to be forgiven. He died bravely, too.'

'How strange,' said Duncan. 'You can never tell what a man is like deep down. I really trusted him... Ah, and here is a man I owe a lot to – more than I can ever pay. Welcome, cousin Macbeth, and thanks!'

'I only did my duty, Your Majesty,' said Macbeth, and bowed.

'You will be well rewarded for being so loyal,' said King Duncan. 'This is a day of great joy,' he went on, turning to everybody, 'and the perfect time for me to make my intentions clear. I declare that my eldest son Malcolm will be King of Scotland after I die, and my other son Donalbain after him...'

Everybody cheered, and Malcolm and Donalbain grinned. But Macbeth realised he had another problem. Even if he killed Duncan, the king's sons stood between him and the crown. But Macbeth made sure his thoughts didn't show on his face and cheered with the others.

'Come, Macbeth, I'll stay with you tonight,' said the king at last. 'That will make our friendship stronger. Your castle is near, isn't it?'

'Yes, Your Majesty,' said Macbeth. 'If you'll allow me, I'll go on ahead to warn my wife you're coming.'

The king gave his permission, and soon Macbeth was riding hard into the night. The castle was quiet when he arrived. Nobody was around except the old gatekeeper, a few guards and Macbeth's wife, Lady Macbeth.

She was waiting for him in their room. A single candle burned. Its light was flickering and unsteady.

'Welcome, great Glamis,' said Lady Macbeth, hugging him. 'But now I must call you Cawdor, too. And you were promised something even greater. Your message made me wonder what the future holds for us.'

'My dearest love,' said Macbeth. 'Duncan is coming here tonight.'

'Is he?' said Lady Macbeth, startled. Then she looked at Macbeth with narrowed eyes. 'Well, I pray he won't see the sun rise tomorrow,' she said.

Macbeth pushed her from him and turned away.

'I know what you're thinking,' whispered Lady Macbeth. 'I can read your face like a book. Well, I've been thinking exactly the same thing.'

'Have you?' said Macbeth. He was shocked to hear her talk about something that had only been a dark thought in his mind. 'But to kill a king is such a terrible crime... I don't know if I can do it.'

'Don't worry,' said Lady Macbeth. 'I'll take care of the planning...'

'Let's not talk about it now,' said Macbeth. 'I need to be alone.'

Later, Macbeth watched from the shadows as Duncan and his men arrived, and Lady Macbeth went out to greet them. Macbeth's mind was full of worry. The Weird Sisters had promised he would be king, and he was certainly ambitious. But there were lots of good reasons not to kill Duncan.

For a start, they were related – the king was Macbeth's cousin. Duncan was a sweet man, and a good king, too. Then there was the murder itself. If only it could be as simple as killing an enemy in battle – one blow that settled everything. But Macbeth knew it would be just the beginning. So many problems might follow...

He met his wife in a passage.

'Where have you been?' said Lady Macbeth, holding up a candle. 'The king has been asking for you.'

'I'm not going to do it,' Macbeth said suddenly. 'This has to stop, right here and right now. The king has been very good to me, and lots of other people think highly of me, and we're doing well enough without... without...'

'What's wrong with you?' snapped Lady Macbeth. 'Are you a man or not? If you want big things in life, you have to be bold and take big risks.'

'Be quiet, woman,' Macbeth snapped back. 'I'm no coward. I'll do anything a man will try.'

'So why did you talk about killing him in the first place?' she said. 'I might be a woman, but I would do it if I had to. I knew you would change your mind. Deep down you're too soft for murder.'

'I'm not, I can do it!' said Macbeth. 'But... but what if we fail?'

'We fail, that's what!' hissed Lady Macbeth. 'But we won't, not if you're as brave as you say. Listen, Duncan hasn't brought bodyguards with him, just two grooms. They'll be sleeping outside his door. I'll make sure they get drunk after the king goes to bed. Then you can do the deed... and we can put the blame on them!'

'Yes, I think it could work...' whispered Macbeth. His eyes glowed, reflecting the candlelight. 'I'll use their daggers. Then I'll cover their clothes and hands with the king's blood...'

'What a wonderful idea!' said Lady Macbeth, smiling. 'If they're found like that, everyone will think they're guilty!'

'So it's settled,' said Macbeth. He clenched his jaw and tried to stay calm. 'Now we'll go to see the king,' he said, 'and keep him happy till he goes to bed. We can put on a good show... but what's in our hearts he'll never know.'

And with that, they walked down the passage into deeper darkness.

Act Two

Death Stalks
the Land

That evening, Macbeth and his wife held a feast for King Duncan and his thanes and servants. The great hall echoed with their loud talk and laughter. At last their bowls and cups were empty, their stomachs full, and it was time for bed.

Banquo and his young son Fleance crossed the castle's gloomy courtyard. They were heading for their room. The night was dark and moonless. The only light came from a few flickering torches.

'Take my sword, Fleance,' said Banquo, handing it to him. 'I'm tired, but I don't really want to go to sleep. I fear I'll have bad dreams as soon as I lay down my head. What time is it, anyway?'

'I'm not sure, Father,' said Fleance. 'But it must be past midnight.'

Suddenly they heard footsteps. A tall, dark figure appeared from the shadows behind them. Banquo was startled, then saw it was Macbeth.

'Still up, my lord?' said Banquo, and smiled. 'The king is long since in bed. He thinks you and Lady Macbeth are wonderful hosts.'

'If only we'd had more time to prepare for him!' said Macbeth.

'Don't worry, everything was fine,' said Banquo. He glanced over his shoulder, and moved in closer to his friend. 'Listen, I can't stop thinking about the Weird Sisters,' he whispered. He let his eyes rest briefly on his son, then looked at Macbeth. 'They spoke some truth to you.'

'I haven't thought about them at all,' Macbeth replied. 'Although I'd be happy to talk about that strange business some time. And remember, you might do very well if we stay friends...'

'So long as that doesn't clash with my other loyalties,' said Banquo, his eyes locked onto Macbeth's. 'Such as to the king.'

'Of course...' said Macbeth. 'Now I won't

keep you any longer. Goodnight to you both.'

Banquo and Fleance went on their way. Macbeth stayed. He thought about what Banquo had said, trying to work out his true meaning. But he soon gave up. He had a job to do. He shook his head, gritted his teeth, and made for the stairs leading to the king's chamber. He put his foot on the first step, then stopped, his eyes wide with shock. A spooky, glowing knife was floating in the air in front of him.

'I don't believe it...' murmured Macbeth. 'Is this a dagger I see before me?' He reached out to touch the handle, but his hand passed through it. Macbeth jumped back as if he had been burned. Was the dagger real, or had it come from his imagination? It was pointing up the stairs, telling him where to go...

Now blood appeared on the knife, too, great blobs of it, and Macbeth realised it wasn't real. He swallowed hard, and felt the night with all its dark magic gathered around him.

A bell rang somewhere, and the dagger vanished. Macbeth took a deep breath... then he started moving up the stairs, slowly and silently...

Lady Macbeth waited in their bedroom. She heard the bell ringing, too. A night bird screeched, and she almost jumped out of her skin.

'Just an owl out hunting...' she whispered, thinking that Death truly stalked the dark land tonight. She had got the grooms drunk, and made sure their daggers were waiting for her husband. She had thought about killing the king herself. But in his sleep he had looked just like her father, and she couldn't do it...

Suddenly Macbeth burst in, the bloodstained daggers in his hands. 'It's done,' he whispered, looking down. He dropped the daggers with a clatter.

'Get a grip on yourself,' said Lady Macbeth, shaking him. 'Listen, if we think too much about what we're doing, we'll drive ourselves mad!'

'I thought I heard someone calling out *sleep no more*,' said Macbeth, ignoring her. '*Macbeth has murdered sleep, the peace that heals us all.*'

'Don't be ridiculous,' snapped Lady Macbeth. 'Nobody said anything. You were imagining it. Here's water to wash your hands. But why did you bring the daggers here? You were supposed to wipe blood on the grooms and leave them there. Quickly, go back and do it.'

'I can't!' groaned Macbeth.

'I will, then,' said Lady Macbeth, and hurried out.

'I'll never wash my hands clean of this blood,' whispered Macbeth. 'Not even if I use an ocean of water. They'd turn the whole sea red...'

Lady Macbeth soon returned. Her hands were now as bloodstained as her husband's. She stood beside Macbeth to wash them. 'You see, it's easy!' she said. 'A little water clears us of what we've done. But wait... what's that?' There was a distant knocking. Someone was banging on the castle gate.

KNOCK! KNOCK! came the sound... KNOCK! KNOCK!

'I wish they could wake Duncan with that knocking...' said Macbeth.

Down in the courtyard, the old gatekeeper shuffled slowly towards the gate. The knocking was growing more regular. KNOCK! KNOCK! A faint, silvery light shone round the edges of the eastern clouds, like the pale ghost of the future. Dawn was approaching.

'All right, all right, I'm on my way,' grumbled the old gatekeeper. 'I've been as busy as the porter at the gates of hell tonight, what with all these comings and goings.

Although I bet I'd be a lot warmer in hell than I am in this freezing castle.' *KNOCK*! *KNOCK*! 'All right, I hear you!'

He opened the gate, and in rode Lennox and Macduff, the Thane of Fife. The men jumped down and marched over to the gatekeeper.

'What took you so long, old man?' said Macduff. 'Were you still in bed? You must have gone to sleep late if you were.'

'Ah, we did,' said the gatekeeper. 'We feasted till the small hours.'

'Is your master up?' said Macduff. Then he saw Macbeth coming through a door. 'Ah, there he is! Our knocking must have woken him.'

'Good morning, Macbeth!' said Lennox. 'Is the king awake?'

'Not yet,' said Macbeth, making sure his face gave nothing away.

'He told me to come for him early, and I was very nearly late,' said Macduff.

He raised his eyebrows at the old gatekeeper, who shrugged.

'Well, better late than never,' said Macbeth. 'I'll take you to him.'

'No, no, you mustn't put yourself out, although I know you don't mind,' said Macduff, smiling. 'Just point me in the right direction.'

'As you wish,' said Macbeth, relieved. 'The door's over there.'

Macbeth watched Macduff cross the courtyard and run up the stairs. He had climbed them himself a few short hours ago, although now it seemed like a lifetime... He remembered how he had left the king, and suddenly felt sick.

'It's been a wild night, hasn't it?' said Lennox. 'The wind was so strong I thought it was going to rip off the roof. There's been talk of the earth shaking, too, and people hearing strange sounds. Someone said they were like the screams of someone dying.'

'Yes,' murmured Macbeth, staring at him. 'It was a rough night.'

Just then they heard footsteps stumbling down the staircase, and they both looked round.

Macduff ran towards them. 'Oh horror, horror, horror...' he groaned. 'I can barely speak of it!'

'Why, what's the matter?' said Macbeth, although he knew full well.

'The king... has been *murdered*!' wailed Macduff.

Lennox gasped, and Macbeth did his best to look shocked, too. 'If you don't believe me, go and see for yourselves,' Macduff went on.

Lennox ran towards the stairs, and Macbeth followed.

'Wake up, everyone!' yelled Macduff. 'Ring the alarm bell!' The old gatekeeper went off to do just that, and the bell's clanging soon rang out. 'Banquo and Donalbain and Malcolm, wake up!'

Soon the castle courtyard began to fill with confused, frightened people in their nightclothes.

Lady Macbeth was one of the first to appear. 'What on earth is going on?' she said.

Banquo and the others were on her heels, and gathered round Macduff.

'I'm… I'm afraid to tell you, my lady,' he said. 'It is too terrible for your delicate ears. Oh, Banquo, the good king has been murdered!'

'What!' Banquo cried out, appalled. There were screams from others in the courtyard. 'I beg you, Macduff…' he moaned. 'Say it isn't so.'

Just then, Macbeth and Lennox returned. They were pale and trembling. Macbeth's face was a mask of horror, and he was only half pretending. 'I wish I had never lived to see this moment,' he said.

Lady Macbeth was watching him, and Banquo was watching them both.

'My life till now was blessed,' Macbeth went on. 'But the best is gone with the king, and nothing good is left, nothing.'

Two young men suddenly pushed through the crowd – Malcolm and Donalbain, the king's sons. 'What is happening here?' said Malcolm.

'The head, the source, the fountain of your family's blood has been cut off!' said Macbeth. He reached out to grasp the young men's shoulders, and tears rolled down his cheeks.

Malcolm and Donalbain looked at each other, confused. They had no idea what he was talking about.

'He means that your father has been murdered,' Macduff said gently.

'But... who would do such a dreadful thing?' muttered Malcolm.

'We're pretty sure it was your father's grooms,' said Lennox, shaking his head. 'They were covered in his blood, and so were their daggers.'

'It's true,' said Macbeth. 'But still, I wish I hadn't killed them.'

'Why did you, then?' yelled Macduff, angrily. 'Now we may never know if they acted alone, or if someone put them up to it!'

'Who could stay calm at a time like this?' Macbeth shouted. 'I saw the king lying there. And I saw his evil, bloodstained murderers, too. I couldn't stop myself.'

Macduff seemed unsatisfied by this answer. He opened his mouth to yell something else. But Lady Macbeth suddenly moaned as if she were about to faint, and he sprang forward to help her instead.

Macbeth stayed where he was. He knew his wife was playing a clever trick. Everyone was looking at her now, and not at him...

'Take care of the lady!' Banquo called out to her servants. Several came forward and took her back inside the castle. 'We should get dressed, then meet to talk about this bloody piece of work,' said Banquo. His strong voice echoed round the courtyard. 'We're all shaken by what's happened, especially as we don't know what lies behind it. But if there is more evil to come, I swear I'll fight it.'

'Me, too!' said Macduff, and everyone else roared in agreement.

Only Macbeth stayed silent – until he saw Banquo staring at him. 'Very well,' said Macbeth, raising his own voice above the noise. 'Let's put on our armour like men, and meet again in the hall!'

The courtyard quickly emptied. Everyone hurried off in different directions. But Malcolm held his brother back, and the two of them stood in a corner to talk. The sun had risen, although thick clouds hung low over Macbeth's castle and made the daylight seem grey and sickly.

'We're not safe here,' whispered Malcolm. 'We can't trust them.'

'You're right,' Donalbain murmured. 'We might be next on the list. We'd better split up and leave the country. I'll go to Ireland.'

'I'll make for England,' said Malcolm. 'And let's not wait around. We'll need the swiftness of our horses to keep us safe and sound.'

So the brothers hugged one last time, and shook each other by the hand. Then they rode away, fleeing through Scotland's darkening land...

Act Three

A Ghost
at Dinner

Strange things happened in the days that followed Duncan's death. The weather was dark and gloomy. The skies over Scotland filled with such thick clouds that noon seemed like midnight, and the whole country felt like a grave. A small owl was seen to kill a great falcon. Then the horses in the royal stables went mad, and ate each other.

Macbeth was crowned king. It didn't take him long to blame Malcolm and Donalbain for Duncan's murder. The fact that they had fled the country made it obvious, said Macbeth – they must have plotted against their father, and bribed the grooms to do the deed. Nobody argued with him. He soon made it pretty clear that no one was allowed to.

Many people were unhappy with the way things had turned out, though. Macduff refused to go to Macbeth's coronation. And Banquo often found himself thinking about Macbeth's sudden run of amazing good luck

– Macbeth had everything the Weird Sisters had promised him. He was Thane of Glamis and Cawdor, and now he was king, too. But was it luck and nothing more?

Banquo had thought about it, and was now convinced that Macbeth had murdered Duncan. Everything pointed to it. And if the Weird Sisters had been right about Macbeth, perhaps the things they had said to him might have some truth in them as well...

Then one day, a messenger came with an order for Banquo to visit the new king. Macbeth was living in Duncan's palace, so Banquo made his way there. He marched down its dark passageways, his mind racing.

Banquo entered the great hall and stood before the king. Macbeth sat on his throne, in rich robes with a golden crown upon his head. Lady Macbeth was on her throne beside him. Lennox and Ross were there, and a crowd of thanes and servants and guards. Banquo tried to keep his face blank. He didn't want to show what he had been thinking.

'Ah, welcome, Banquo,' said Macbeth. Banquo bowed low. Macbeth stood up and came over to him. 'We're having a dinner party tonight,' he said, taking his friend's arm. 'I'd like you to be one of the guests.'

'Oh, do say you will, Banquo, please,' said Lady Macbeth. 'It won't be the same without you.'

'Your wish is my command, Your Royal Majesties,' Banquo replied.

'Wonderful!' said Macbeth. He gave him a big smile. But Banquo noticed the king's eyes were cold. 'Tell me, old friend, are you going riding this afternoon?'

Banquo nodded.

'That's a shame. I was hoping you'd be here for my council meeting. You know how much I value your advice. He leaned closer to Banquo. 'Have you heard what Malcolm and Donalbain are up to?' he whispered. 'They're claiming they didn't kill their father, and they're spreading all sorts of wild stories. But we can talk about that tomorrow. Are you taking Fleance riding with you?'

'I am, my lord,' said Banquo. 'And we really should get going...'

'Fine, off you go then, old friend!' said Macbeth, smiling again as Banquo left. 'And I'll say goodbye to everyone else until this evening, too. I'll enjoy the party more if I have some time alone now.'

The great hall emptied. Lady Macbeth glanced at her husband with a curious expression as she left. Macbeth ignored her, and called over one of the servants. 'Are those men still waiting?' he whispered.

'Yes, my lord,' the servant replied. 'They're outside, at the gate.'

'Bring them to me,' hissed Macbeth, and the servant hurried away.

Macbeth sat thinking, his face dark. He didn't feel secure as king. He had talked to his wife about it. Banquo was a friend, but also a threat. He was brave and clever, a man who knew how to get his own way. Look how he'd taken charge of things after Duncan's body had been discovered! Besides, the Weird Sisters had promised Banquo's children would be kings, not Macbeth's – if he ever had any.

Macbeth knew that he had ruined his peace of mind for ever by murdering Duncan. But he hadn't done it simply to hand over the crown to Banquo's children when he died. No, that wasn't going to happen. Not if he could possibly help it. For he too was a man who knew how to get his own way...

The servant soon returned, bringing two rough-looking men with him. Macbeth dismissed the servant and drew the men into a dark corner.

'Have you thought about what I said yesterday?' Macbeth whispered. Both men stared at him. They shuffled their feet. 'You understand that it was Banquo who plotted

against you and held you back, don't you?'
said Macbeth. 'It was Banquo who made sure
you and your families would be poor for ever.
What are you going to do about it?'

Of course, none of this was true. Macbeth
had made up these lies to get the men to hate
Banquo. He knew that would make it easier
to get them to do what he wanted.

'Why, we... we won't stand for it, my lord,'
said one of them at last. He looked at the
other man, and then at Macbeth. 'We are
men, after all.'

'I suppose you count as men... of a sort,'
said Macbeth, looking them up and down.
'But both mongrels and fine hounds are
called dogs. Convince me that you're *real*
men, and I'll give you a job that will solve
your problem as well as mine.'

'We've lived hard lives, my lord,' said the
second man. 'And we'll do whatever it takes
to revenge ourselves on those who have done
us down.'

'Good,' said Macbeth. He smiled, pleased that his plan had worked. 'Banquo is my enemy just as much as he is yours. I could use my power as king to have him executed. But that would upset some of our friends. So I would rather, well... keep it quiet. That's why I'm asking for your help...'

'Just tell us what you want done, my lord,' said the first man.

'Banquo must die tonight,' said Macbeth. 'And make sure that his son Fleance dies with him. The boy's death is as important to me as his father's. Is that clear?'

The men said it was, and Macbeth sent them away.

Soon after, Lady Macbeth returned to the great hall. 'What's wrong, dear husband?' she asked, her voice full of concern. 'Why have you been spending so much time on your own? There's no point in dwelling on the past. What's done is done.'

'But we haven't finished the job,' said

Macbeth, turning from her. 'And we're in danger till we do. That's why we've both been having terrible dreams every night. The dead don't dream though, do they? They don't ever have to worry again...'

'Please, stop torturing yourself!' said Lady Macbeth, holding his arm. 'Just stay calm, and put on a good face for your guests tonight.'

'I will, even though my mind is full of evil,' said Macbeth. 'And I hope you can do the same. Remember to be especially nice about Banquo. It's important no one knows how we really feel about him. A dreadful deed is to be done tonight, at dusk...'

'What... what is going to happen?' whispered Lady Macbeth, her eyes wide with fear. She held a trembling hand to her pale cheek.

'Never you mind, my love,' said Macbeth. 'You'll find out soon enough. Come on, let's get ready for the party...' And he led her away to their private rooms.

Meanwhile, Banquo and Fleance were riding happily through the woods. They were enjoying their time together, not knowing it would soon be cut short. As the dying sun lit the gloomy clouds with orange fire, father and son came trotting down the road towards the palace.

Suddenly, two dark figures appeared in front of them. Banquo saw a flash of steel and realised they were being attacked! The men made a grab for the horses' reins. Banquo pulled in front of his son, and drew his sword at the same time. But Banquo's horse reared, and he was thrown to the ground.

'Escape, Fleance! Run for your life!' he yelled, as the men jumped on him. They stabbed him with their blades before he could get to his feet and fight them off.

Fleance didn't need to be told twice. He turned his horse, and galloped back the way they had come.

'This one is taken care of,' said the first

man. He kicked the blood-covered corpse of Banquo. 'But the boy still lives, worse luck.'

'You're right, blast it,' muttered the second man. He wiped his dagger clean on his sleeve. 'Come on, we'd better go and tell Macbeth...'

A short while later, Macbeth and his wife greeted their guests as they took their seats in the royal dining room. 'Welcome to you all!' boomed Macbeth. He walked round the table shaking hands, patting backs, playing the friendly host. Then he caught sight of one of the men he'd sent to murder Banquo slipping in quietly.

Macbeth hurried over and pulled the man to one side, making sure his guests couldn't see him. 'There's blood on your face,' he hissed nervously.

'It's Banquo's,' replied the man, wiping it on his sleeve.

'Is he dead?' said Macbeth.

'My lord, we left him lying in a ditch with twenty mortal wounds...' whispered the man. 'Any single one of them would have killed him. But we cut his throat, just to make sure.'

'I'm pleased to hear it,' said Macbeth. 'What about Fleance?'

'I'm sorry, my lord...' said the man, hesitating. 'Fleance escaped.'

'That's bad news,' muttered Macbeth. He bit his lip. 'My day would have been perfect otherwise. Ah well, at least we've got rid of the grown-up snake. The young one might be full of venom some day, but he can't hurt me yet...'

Macbeth dismissed the man and walked back to his guests. But his face was troubled.

Lady Macbeth frowned. 'We can't get started till you give the toast, my lord,' she said brightly.

All eyes turned to Macbeth. No one noticed a strange, ghostly figure drift into the room and take the last empty seat at the table...

'You're right, of course,' said Macbeth, pulling himself together. He picked up a gold cup and raised it high. 'Come, let's enjoy this wonderful food. I wish you good health! How marvellous to see so many good friends here. If only Banquo were with us!'

'He's the one who's missing out, Your Majesty, not us,' laughed Ross. 'Please, take your seat, my lord.'

'But the table is already full,' said Macbeth, puzzled.

'No, here is your place, my lord,' said Lennox, pointing at the empty seat.

Macbeth looked – and stepped back, horrified. He dropped his gold cup with a loud clatter, and groaned. The bloodstained ghost of Banquo was sitting in his place. His gaping gashes oozed blood, and his eyes glowed red.

'What the...' Macbeth moaned. 'Which of you has done this?' The ghost slowly shook his head, and raised a finger to point at

Macbeth. 'I swear I didn't,' Macbeth muttered. 'Don't stare at me like that.'

'What's wrong, my lord?' Lennox said, uneasily. There was a murmur of alarm around the table. The ghost remained invisible to everyone except Macbeth. Ross and some of the others rose to their feet.

'Please, don't be worried,' said Lady Macbeth. She stood up and went to Macbeth's side. 'The king has had these... little fits... all his life. It will pass, and he will soon be himself again.' She pulled him away from the table. 'What do you think you're doing?' she whispered fiercely. 'You're behaving like a frightened child, not a man...'

'But I am a man,' whispered Macbeth. He couldn't stop staring at the ghost. 'One bold enough to look at something that might scare the devil.'

'What are you talking about?' hissed Lady Macbeth. 'Nothing is there. It's just a chair!'

'But *he* is there!' said Macbeth. He pulled her head round roughly. The ghost smiled and nodded, but Lady Macbeth couldn't see anything. 'In the old days you could murder someone and they would stay dead,' Macbeth muttered. 'But now if you cut someone's throat and send him to hell, he comes straight back to take your seat!'

'My lord, our guests are watching...' Lady Macbeth whispered.

'I know,' he moaned. He tore his eyes away from the ghost at last. 'My friends, please forgive me,' he said. 'Let's have another toast. Give me some wine. Love and health to all!' He picked up his cup again, and his guests raised theirs, uncertainly. Then Macbeth turned... and saw Banquo again. 'Get away!' Macbeth screamed. He threw his cup at him, but it passed straight through, and the ghost just laughed.

The other people round the table were very spooked now. They were all on their feet, most of them backing away. Lennox and Ross glanced at each other.

'Listen, everybody, please!' shouted Lady Macbeth at last. 'I'm afraid I must ask you all to leave! Forgive us, but... but the king's fits sometimes grow worse when there are too many people around...' She hurried everyone out of the chamber and returned to her husband.

Macbeth was sitting at the table with his head in his hands. He looked up when he heard her. He was relieved to see that the ghost had vanished.

'Blood will have blood, they say,' he murmured. 'But I have waded so far into a sea of blood, it would be just as hard to turn back now, as it would be to keep going. And we have another problem. I've heard that Macduff is refusing to have anything to do with me...'

'How do you know that?' said Lady Macbeth, surprised.

'I have spies in the houses of all my enemies,' said Macbeth. 'Don't worry; I have a plan for dealing with him. And soon I will go to see the Weird Sisters again. I need to find out what else they can tell me.'

'What you need is some sleep, my lord,' said Lady Macbeth.

'Yes, perhaps the ghost was only in my head,' said Macbeth, deep in thought, 'and will not dare to visit us when we're in our bed...'

But as they left the room, neither of them really believed it.

Act Four

The Storm Clouds Gather

A few days later, two riders met by a lonely lake. The grey water glinted in the weak winter sun. The men got off their horses and shook hands, then moved from the road into the cover of a wood.

'I think it's safe to talk here,' said Lennox, one of the men. 'You just can't be too careful these days. Are you sure you weren't followed?'

'Of course,' said Ross, although he still looked over his shoulder.

'That's good,' murmured Lennox, relaxing. 'Listen, I know we both feel the same about what's been going on. It's strange how so many bad things have happened to people with links to... a certain person.'

'A certain *villain*, you mean,' growled Ross. 'You're right. King Duncan stays with him for one night and is murdered. Then Banquo is invited to dinner at the palace and ends up murdered, too.'

'Let's not be afraid to use the villain's

name,' said Lennox. 'We know it all comes back to Macbeth. And the latest news is that our murdering king is out to get Macduff. Have you any idea where Macduff is?'

'At the court of the English king, with Malcolm,' said Ross. 'He's gone south to join the fight against Macbeth, leaving his wife and children in Fife. Of course, Macbeth is furious. He says that Malcolm and Donalbain and their supporters are rebels, and he's preparing for war.'

'So are we all,' said Lennox, his face grim. 'I never thought I'd say this, but let's hope the day will soon come when we are free of him. Someone should go to Malcolm and Macduff. We need to let them know that many of us are ready to help.'

'I'll do that,' said Ross. They shook hands, got back on their horses, and rode off on their separate ways, Lennox to his castle, Ross to England...

That night, in the small hours, Macbeth

rose quietly from his bed. He threw a dark, hooded cloak round his shoulders and made for the door, pausing briefly to look back at his wife. She lay, restless and groaning, her mind full of bad dreams. He sighed, then turned and left the room. He hurried through the sleeping palace and out to the stables.

Moments later, he was riding hard, heading for the lonely crossroads where he had first seen the Weird Sisters. A full moon was high in the sky. Its silver light cast long shadows, among them a ghostly horse that seemed to gallop beside him...

The Weird Sisters took no notice of him when he arrived. They were huddled round a fire with a large metal cooking pot hanging over it.

Macbeth stopped his horse and jumped down. He stood watching the women for a moment. Huge storm clouds started to gather. Lightning flickered and flashed, and thunder rumbled.

The Weird Sisters were chanting. Their voices were harsh, and the sound rose and fell. Two of them threw strange things into the pot, while the third stirred the steaming brew with a long, metal spoon...

Double, double, toil and trouble,
Fire burn and cauldron bubble.
Eye of newt and toe of frog,
Wool of bat and tongue of dog,
For a charm of powerful trouble,
Like a hell-broth, boil and bubble...

Macbeth moved towards them, and the nearest woman turned round.

'By the pricking of my thumbs, something wicked this way comes,' she muttered, and all three cackled.

Macbeth stopped in his tracks, his heart pounding. Then he walked on, determined not to be scared. 'We meet once more...' he whispered. 'Answer *all* my questions this time.

Tell me everything I want to know.'

'Well then, ask away...' said the first Sister, giving a little shrug.

'And you will have answers...' said the second Sister, smiling.

'But not from us...' said the third Sister, her eyes narrowed.

'Call whatever spirits you like,' said Macbeth. 'I'm ready.'

The Weird Sisters started chanting and throwing things into the pot again. *Double, double, toil and trouble, fire burn and cauldron bubble...*

On the last word, there was a flash, and a terrifying sight appeared – the ghostly head of a warrior, complete with horned helmet. The head floated right in front of Macbeth, who gulped and opened his mouth to speak... but the third Sister quickly held up her hand.

'He knows what you're thinking,' she said. 'Just listen.'

'Macbeth, Macbeth,' wailed the head, 'beware Macduff, the Thane of Fife...'

'Thanks for the warning, but I'd worked that out for myself,' muttered Macbeth. Then he noticed that the head was beginning to fade away. 'Wait, don't go, tell me more!'

'He won't be ordered around,' said the second Sister with a cackle. 'The next spirit comes... Beware! This one is even more powerful.'

The head vanished, and there was another, bigger flash. A blood-covered baby appeared, and floated in the air like the head. Macbeth felt the hairs prickling on the back of his neck, but he stayed where he was. He waited for the baby to speak, while thunder rumbled above.

'Be bloodthirsty, bold and resolute,' wailed the baby at last. 'For no man born of a woman shall harm you, Macbeth.'

Macbeth closed his eyes for a second, and breathed in deeply. He was filled with relief. All men were born of women, so, if this spirit spoke truly, he need not fear Macduff, or anyone else. He breathed out and opened his eyes, and saw that the baby had vanished.

'And now the last spirit comes,' said the first Sister. 'Behold...'

The flash was the biggest yet, and dazzled Macbeth. An even stranger figure appeared this time. A small child, wearing a crown and holding a branch, was floating in the air.

Macbeth watched and waited, feeling the magic crackle around him.

'Fear not those who plot against you, Macbeth,' moaned the child, its voice like a grown man's. 'For you will never be defeated. Not till Great Burnam Wood comes marching to attack you on high Dunsinane Hill.'

Macbeth frowned. He was puzzled by the spirit's words. His old castle stood on Dunsinane Hill. He planned to use it as a base should Malcolm bring his army to Scotland. And Burnam Wood was a forest that stood nearby. Then Macbeth smiled.

A forest couldn't pull up its roots and attack a castle, could it? Which meant he would always be safe there...

'Thank you, spirit,' he said as the child vanished. 'And I thank you, too, Weird Sisters. I have the answers to almost all my questions. There's just one last thing... Will the children of Banquo ever rule this kingdom?'

'Ah, seek not to know that!' wailed The Weird Sisters together.

'I *must* know,' roared Macbeth. 'May you be cursed for ever if you do not tell me. But wait, what are you doing? What's happening?'

The fire and the cauldron had suddenly vanished, and the Weird Sisters had stood up and turned to face him. A huge flash of lightning lit the scene, and a great clap of thunder boomed directly above. Macbeth covered his eyes and fell to his knees.

'Come, shadow kings, now make a start,' wailed the first Sister.

'We conjure you with our magic art,' wailed the second Sister.

'Show Macbeth, and grieve his heart...' wailed the third Sister.

Then the ghost of Banquo appeared and stood beside his old friend. Banquo waved somebody forward, and Macbeth saw a line of phantoms emerge from the darkness, eight future kings walking past, one after another. The first one was Fleance. Banquo smiled and pointed to himself to make sure that Macbeth understood.

Macbeth groaned and hung his head, and the Weird Sisters cackled and danced around him. He felt dizzy and sick. The movement and noise grew to a climax until he thought he could stand no more...

Then suddenly it stopped, and Macbeth looked up. He was alone. The Weird Sisters, Banquo and the future kings had all disappeared. Macbeth rose slowly to his feet. He got on his horse and rode off, grimly.

So be it, he thought as his horse's hooves drummed on the road. The future might belong to Banquo's children... But he, Macbeth, was the king here and now, in the present. And from this moment on he would be even more cruel and ruthless than ever. He would do whatever it took to hold on to power. And he knew just where he was going to start, too.

Macduff had joined the rebels – well, his family would pay the price...

A few days later, a band of hard-faced men surrounded Macduff's castle. They burst in through the gates and quickly overcame the few guards Macduff had left. They found his wife in her private rooms with her youngest son. She backed against the wall, holding on to him.

'What is the meaning of this?' she said, angrily. 'Who are you?'

'Never you mind that, my lady,' muttered one of the men. 'Your husband is a traitor, and we've come to take the king's revenge.'

'My father's not a traitor, you are!' yelled the boy, but it was too late.

Blades flashed and blood flowed, and screams filled the air. Macbeth's men left the bodies where they had fallen, and burnt down the castle. They rode away, laughing, satisfied with the job they had done. One single servant escaped, and went to Lennox with a tale of horror and death. Lennox sent a message to the rebels.

Macduff was with Malcolm and Donalbain, helping them to organise an army to go back to Scotland.

'Tell me, Macduff,' said Malcolm as they rode out one morning. 'Why did you leave your wife and children at home? Surely they're not safe.'

'It was a risk I had to take,' Macduff replied. 'A warriors' camp is no place for a family. But I know it made some people suspicious of me.'

'I've had a few doubts about you myself,' murmured Malcolm. 'What if you've struck a deal with Macbeth? Perhaps he's agreed not to harm your family if you do something for him in return. Such as kill me...'

'You can trust me, my lord,' said Macduff. 'I am not a traitor.'

Malcolm turned in his saddle to look at him, and smiled. 'I know, Macduff,' he said. 'You are what you appear to be, a good man. Not like Macbeth, who seemed good, and revealed himself to be evil. But perhaps I am more like him than you. I have many, many faults.'

'You can't possibly be as evil as Macbeth,' said Macduff, shaking his head.

'You don't know that,' said Malcolm. 'Great power changes men. If I become king, it might bring out the greed and violence in me. Then poor Scotland could end up being ruled by someone far worse than Macbeth.'

'Well in that case,' said Macduff, stopping his horse and staring at Malcolm with narrowed eyes, 'I would want nothing more to do with you. I will not serve another evil ruler, whoever his father was.'

Malcolm stopped his horse beside Macduff and smiled at him once more. 'Forgive me for making you angry, Macduff,' he said. 'But I was testing you and you gave me exactly the right answer. I love truth and goodness as I love life itself. All that matters to me is freeing our country from Macbeth. Give me your hand and we'll do it together!'

Macduff smiled, too, but then they heard the sound of hooves on the road behind them. A rider appeared, and they saw it was Ross.

'Welcome, Ross,' said Malcolm. 'Have you news for us from home?'

'Yes, my lord, and none of it good,' said Ross, his face grim.

'That's no surprise,' said Malcolm. 'Well then, what's the latest grief?'

'I dread to tell you,' said Ross, glancing at Macduff and looking away.

'Is it... something to do with my family?' said Macduff. The colour drained from his cheeks. 'If it is, don't keep it from me, man!'

'Forgive me for bringing this news to you, Macduff,' said Ross. 'But Macbeth ordered your castle to be attacked, and everyone in it killed.'

'What, my family... murdered?' said Macduff, horrified. 'My wife and... and all my children, too?'

Ross nodded, and Macduff staggered. Malcolm and Ross quickly moved to help him. But Macduff shook them off and steadied himself.

'You know what to do, Macduff.' Malcolm said quietly. 'You need to get back at Macbeth. Be a man... and take your revenge.'

'Oh, don't worry, I will,' said Macduff, turning to Malcolm. His face was furious, his eyes full of tears. 'Now all I want is to have Macbeth at the tip of my sword.'

'That's what I want to hear,' said Malcolm. 'A grief like yours will always smart, and help to keep your anger burning fiercely in your heart.' Then he clapped both Macduff and Ross on their backs. 'Our army is ready at last, my friends,' he said. 'And it's long past time... to attack!'

Act Five

The Final
Battle

Malcolm rode north at the head of a great army that spring, with Macduff by his side. The English king had lent them many warriors. As soon as Malcolm crossed the border, the Scottish thanes rose against Macbeth, bringing their men to the fight, too. And for a time it seemed that the gates of hell had opened wide on the suffering people and their country.

Arrows swished through the air, sword clanged on sword, and men screamed and bled and died. Macbeth had plenty of warriors. But they were men who fought for money, not because they believed in his right to be king. The kind of men who were happy to kill innocent people and burn their villages. And that made the people hate Macbeth even more.

Macbeth moved back to his old castle on Dunsinane Hill, and made it as strong as he could. But strange things happened inside it, just as they had done at the royal palace.

One night, when everyone should have been sleeping but the guards on the walls, a doctor came to Lady Macbeth's private rooms. He knocked quietly, and a maid opened the door. She held her finger to her lips and let him in, closing the door behind them. A candle cast a flickering light, and shadows danced in the corners.

'Tell me again about this… sleepwalking,' whispered the doctor.

'It started when the fighting began,' the maid replied. 'The queen would get out of bed, walk around for a while talking to herself, then get back into bed. And all the time she would be asleep.'

'Very odd,' said the doctor. 'What did she actually say?'

'I… I can't tell you,' said the maid, suddenly uneasy. 'She spoke about things that have happened. But no one else was there to hear her, so I can't prove it. And I don't want to get into trouble. But wait, here she comes!'

An inner door creaked open, and Lady Macbeth came out of her bedroom. She walked past the doctor and the maid, ignoring them.

'Her eyes are wide open, but she obviously can't see us...' whispered the doctor. 'And why is she rubbing her hands?'

'She does that a lot, even when she's awake,' said the maid. 'I've seen her do it for a quarter of an hour at a time. It's as if she's washing them.'

'Here's another spot!' moaned Lady Macbeth. She looked at her hands, and rubbed them crazily. 'Who would have thought the old man had so much blood in him?'

The doctor drew a sharp breath and glanced at the maid. 'Did you hear that?' he hissed. But the maid put her finger to her lips again.

'The Thane of Fife had a wife. Where is she now?' said Lady Macbeth in a singsong voice.

Then she sighed. 'And here's the smell of blood still. All the perfume in the world will not sweeten this little hand of mine...' She talked of Banquo's death, and the deaths of many others, and finally she went back to bed.

'You'd better keep an eye on her,' said the doctor. 'And make sure she doesn't harm herself. I'll tell the king...'

The doctor hurried through the castle, then crossed the courtyard. It was now filled with the noise of warriors getting ready for battle. Men shouted and horses neighed. Macbeth was in the hall with his hard-faced warriors. Messengers came in with reports, and left with his orders.

'Bring me my armour, Seyton,' Macbeth yelled. Seyton was his personal body servant. 'Is there any more news?'

'You've heard it all already, my lord,' said Seyton. He hurried over to the king. 'And I don't think you need to put on your armour just yet.'

'Well, I do!' roared Macbeth. Seyton quickly got to work. Just then, Macbeth saw the doctor enter the hall. 'How is she, doctor? Still sick?'

'I wouldn't call it a sickness, my lord,' the doctor said. 'Her mind seems to be full of bad thoughts. That's why she can't sleep.'

'Don't you have anything to cure her?' said Macbeth. 'Some drug to calm her brain?'

'Alas no, my lord,' murmured the doctor. 'It's the kind of problem you can only solve for yourself.'

'Hang your medicine then!' roared Macbeth. He shivered as if someone had walked across his grave. For a moment he felt certain there would be no quiet future for him, either. But why should he worry? Burnam Wood would never come to Dunsinane. And he couldn't be killed by any man born of a woman... Seyton buckled his breastplate, then Macbeth put on his horned helmet and picked up his shield. The doubts went away. 'Although I don't suppose you've got a drug to get rid of these rebels, have you, doctor?' he said, and his warriors laughed.

'Er... I'm afraid not, my lord,' said the doctor.

Macbeth grinned. 'Not to worry,' he said, striding out of the hall. 'I can deal with them!'

The doctor watched him go, shaking his head. He thought about escaping from Macbeth's castle. It seemed like a wise thing to do...

Malcolm's army, meanwhile, was approaching. The sky was blue, but half full of fluffy, white clouds that hid the sun. Their shadows moved swiftly over the warriors below. Suddenly Malcolm raised his hand. His army came to a halt at the edge of a thick forest.

'What is this wood called?' he said.

'Why, Burnam Wood, my lord,' said one of his men. 'Macbeth's castle lies beyond it, on Dunsinane Hill. But we can't be seen from here.'

'That's good,' said Malcolm. 'I don't want the villain to know how big my army is yet. So this is what we'll do. I want every man to cut a branch from a tree and hold it before him as we march on the castle. That way our numbers will be concealed, and we'll have surprise on our side!'

Later that morning, Macbeth strode out into the courtyard. He was pleased with the way things were going. 'This castle is too strong for Malcolm,' he said, grinning. 'He and his men can sit outside my walls for as long as they like, but they'll never get in.'

Suddenly, there was the sound of women screaming. Macbeth whirled round, startled. 'What is that noise?' he said.

'It was the cry of Lady Macbeth's maids, my lord,' said a wide-eyed Seyton, running up to him. 'The queen... has killed herself.'

Macbeth turned away, and looked up at

the sky. She was too young to die, he thought. But what did it matter? What did anything matter? Time moved on from day to day, and Death waited for us all in the end. Living was like being an actor on a stage. Someone who struts and talks and vanishes, never to be seen again. Life was a tale told by an idiot, full of sound and fury, and meant nothing...

Macbeth looked round at last. He saw that another messenger was waiting. This one seemed nervous, his eyes even wider than Seyton's.

'Well then?' snapped Macbeth. 'What have you got to tell me?'

'I don't know how to say it, my lord...' said the messenger. 'I was on guard duty, watching from the walls, and I thought I saw...'

'Speak up, man!' yelled Macbeth. 'For heaven's sake, spit it out!'

'I thought I saw Burnam Wood begin to move,' said the messenger.

'You're a liar!' roared Macbeth, grabbing the man by the throat. 'And you'll be a dead liar, too, if you're trying to upset me. I'll have you hanged and your body left dangling till the flesh falls from your bones.'

'I'm not, I swear!' said the messenger. 'Go and see for yourself!'

Macbeth raced up to the castle wall. He looked out across the land... and suddenly felt his blood run cold. A great mass of green was coming towards him. 'You will never be defeated...' he muttered to himself. 'Not till Great Burnam Wood comes marching to attack you on high Dunsinane Hill.'

And now it was doing just that...

Had the Weird Sisters and the spirits tricked him? Was everything else they said lies, too? Well, whatever the truth, there was only one way to deal with it – like a man. Macbeth squared his shoulders and set his jaw. He didn't care if Death was waiting for him, so long as their meeting place could be on the battlefield. 'Open the gates!' he yelled. 'Come on, lads, let's show these rebel weaklings what we're made of!'

Soon Macbeth was thundering down the hill on his horse at the head of his army. He roared boldly, and the sunlight flashed off his sword...

'Throw away your branches now,' Malcolm said calmly. 'It's time to fight. Good luck to you all, and death to the villain Macbeth!'

Malcolm's army rushed forward. The ground shook as the men raced towards each other, and they met with a great *CRASH*! Blades clanged on blades and helmets and shields. Arrows flew, horses screamed and kicked, men hacked and stabbed and bled and died.

Macbeth fought like a demon. 'No man born of woman can kill me!' he yelled – even though deep inside he was no longer sure it was true. But he was still a fierce and skilful warrior, and it did seem that no man could stand up to him. His sword cut through Malcolm's warriors like a knife through water.

Macduff searched for Macbeth. He wouldn't fight anyone other than the man who had murdered his family. 'I'd rather put my sword back in its sheath unused than kill one of these pathetic men you pay to fight for you, Macbeth,' he muttered to himself amid the din...

Then, suddenly, he heard a much greater noise coming from a part of the battlefield. That's where Macbeth would be, where the fight was hottest... Macduff ran towards the sound, his sword raised.

Macbeth was pulling his own sword from yet another dead warrior when he heard a harsh voice behind him.

'Turn, hellhound, turn!' it said.

Macbeth looked round. Macduff was staring at him, his eyes glittering with hate.

It went strangely quiet around them, and it seemed as if they were the only two men on the battlefield.

'Get away from me, Macduff,' Macbeth murmured. 'I don't want to fight you. I've got far too much blood of yours on my hands already.'

'And I've got nothing more to say to you, foul villain,' said Macduff, moving in closer. 'I'll let my sword do the talking for me!'

Then he rushed at Macbeth, and a mighty fight began. Macduff struck with all his fury. But Macbeth held off every blow, and fought back fiercely. Sparks flew as steel clanged on steel. After a while, they paused. Their chests were heaving, and sweat dripped from their cheeks.

'You're... not... really... getting... anywhere, are you?' said Macbeth, panting. He smiled broadly. 'But I could have told you it was a bad idea to fight me. A spirit promised me that no man born of woman could ever kill me, Macduff. You might as well give up trying now.'

'I… don't… think… so,' said Macduff, leaning on his sword. Then he did something Macbeth hadn't been expecting. Macduff smiled, too. 'You see, I wasn't born like other men,' said Macduff. 'My mother died when she was giving birth to me… and I was cut out of her womb.'

Macbeth's blood ran cold. So that's the way it worked, he thought. The spirits hadn't lied. They simply hadn't told him the whole truth, and he'd believed only what he'd wanted to believe. Foul was fair and fair was foul, it seemed…

'I curse you for telling me so,' Macbeth muttered. 'It has made me lose my courage. It's over, I won't fight you.'

'Give up then, you coward,' said Macduff, sneering. 'We'll put you on show like the monster you are, and charge people to look at you.'

'Oh no, you won't,' said Macbeth. He scowled and pulled himself together. 'I'll not be laughed at by some mob, and I won't kiss the ground at Malcolm's feet, either. So what if Burnam Wood came to Dunsinane and you're not born of a woman? I'll give it one last try. Bring it on, Macduff… and damned be either of us if we cry stop, enough!'

Macbeth charged forward with a great, final roar, his sword raised.

Macduff crashed into him halfway, and the fight raged more fiercely than before. But Macduff was the stronger man, and killed the villain with a sweeping stroke. Macbeth's head flew from his body.

At that moment Malcolm arrived, with Lennox and Ross and a host of other thanes and warriors. The battle was over – Macbeth's men beaten, the castle taken. Macduff picked up Macbeth's head and held it high.

'Hail, King Malcolm!' he said. 'Hail, the new King of Scotland!'

Everyone joined in. Malcolm's army roared their approval and banged their shields with their swords. The clouds had gone, and the sun shone down from a sky of blue, on a king who was good, and wise, and true.

And so ends this story of darkness and death, the tale of a man called... *Macbeth*!

About the Author

Tony Bradman was born in London and still lives there. He has written a large number of books for children of all ages, including 25 titles about his most popular creation, Dilly the Dinosaur. Dilly the Dinosaur was made into a long-running TV series and one of the books was shortlisted for the Children's Book Award. Tony has also edited many anthologies of poetry and short stories.

Tony loves reading and going to see Shakespeare plays performed at the restored Globe Theatre on London's South Bank. He thinks Shakespeare is the greatest writer of all time, and his favourite plays are *Macbeth*, of course, and *The Tempest*.

Other White Wolves Shakespeare...

ROMEO & JULIET

retold by Michael Cox

Trouble's brewing on the roughest estate in Nottingham. Romeo Montague has fallen for Juliet Capulet. Big time. But their families hate each other's guts. Worse still, Romeo has just killed Juliet's cousin in a street fight and must leave town quick. What's needed now is a clever plan...

Romeo and Juliet is a modern retelling of a tragic Shakespeare play.

ISBN: 978 0 7136 8136 9   £4.99

Other White Wolves Shakespeare...

The Tempest

retold by **Franzeska G. Ewart**

A year has passed, and Ariel is
remembering the events of that magical
day. The day she conjured a tempest
for her master, the great magician
Prospero, to shipwreck his enemy.
The day love blossomed, fools were
exposed, and traitors brought to justice.
The day everything changed...

The Tempest is a modern retelling of
a magical Shakespeare play.

ISBN: 978 0 7136 7751 5   £4.99

Year 5

The Path of Finn McCool • Sally Prue

The Barber's Clever Wife • Narinder Dhami

Taliesin • Maggie Pearson

Fool's Gold • David Calcutt

Time Switch • Steve Barlow and Steve Skidmore

Let's Go to London! • Kaye Umansky

Year 6

Shock Forest and Other Stories • Margaret Mahy

Sky Ship and Other Stories • Geraldine McCaughrean

Snow Horse and Other Stories • Joan Aiken

Macbeth • Tony Bradman

Romeo and Juliet • Michael Cox

The Tempest • Franzeska G. Ewart